IRL

52%

LOADING

IN REAL LIFE

Cory Doctorow
Jen Wang

New York

For Alice, as always, my kickass
girl gamer and personal zombie-slayer.

—C.D.

Thanks to Judy Hansen, Jake Mumm,
and Yu Fong Wang.

—J.W.

HAIRY
LONGPO TUSK
+15 GOLD

INVENTORY
HAIRY LONGPO TUSK
LOBOK
SKY ELIXIR
CATSEYE
PINECONE
BEACH STONE
ANTS NEST
OMUSUBI
THYME

INTRODUCTION

by Cory Doctorow

In Real Life is a book about games and economics. A lot of us pay attention to games, but think of them as trivial—mere amusements that help us fill the long, dismal stretch between the cradle and the grave. As for economics, well, yeah, people think economics is important, but it's also one of those intimidating no-go areas that scares people away, despite the fact that economics—the study of why people do things, really—is the subject that has the most to say about the circumstances in which they find themselves.

When you put economics and games together, you suddenly find yourself in the middle of a bunch of sticky, tough questions about politics and labor. *In Real Life* connects the dots between the way we shop, the way we organize, and the way we play, and why some people are rich, some are poor, and how they seem to get stuck there.

I hope that readers of this book will be inspired to dig deeper into the subject of behavioral economics and to start asking hard questions about how we end up with the stuff we own, what it costs our human brothers and sisters to make those goods, and why we think we need them.

But it's a poor politics that can only be expressed by choosing to buy or not buy something. Sometimes (often!), you need to organize to make a difference.

This is the golden age of organizing. If there's one thing the Internet's changed forever, it's the relative difficulty and cost of getting a bunch of people in the same place, working toward the same goal. That's not always good (thugs, bullies, racists, and loonies never had it so good), but it is fundamentally *game-changing*.

It's hard to remember just how difficult this organizing stuff used to be: how hard it was to do something as trivial as getting ten friends to agree on dinner and a movie, let alone getting millions of people together to raise money for a political candidate, get the vote out, protest corruption, or save an endangered and beloved institution.

When I was an activist in the 1980s, ninety-eight percent of my time was spent stuffing envelopes and writing addresses on them. The remaining two percent was the time we spent figuring out what to put in the envelopes. Today, we get those envelopes and stamps and address books for free. This is so fantastically, hugely different and weird that we haven't even begun to feel the first tendrils of it. Moments like the Occupy movement and the Gezi uprising in Istanbul will be remembered as the tiniest tremors of what happens when people can organize more cheaply.

Working together is the secret origin story of our species. We diverged from our hominid ancestors when we started to divide up labor—you watch the kids, I'll watch for tigers, and that guy's going to go and forage for fruit. The most modern part of our brains, the neocortex (the "new bark," which wraps around all the more ancient parts of our

brains), developed around this time and is strongly implicated in managing our social relationships. Everything from language and literacy to corporations and countries are just structures for organizing human labor.

The games we play with other people all tickle this organizing mechanism. When you play hide and seek, you try and outguess where your opponents will look (or where they'll hide when they're trying to out outguess you!). When you do a mass raid on some huge instance in an MMO (a massively multiplayer online game), the "game" isn't just killing the boss, it's figuring out how to convince a couple

dozen of your friends to work with you, coordinating your schedules so that you can raid together, agreeing on tactics, even coming up with a chain of command and hammering out its legitimacy.

It's not surprising that gamespace has become a workplace for hundreds of thousands of "gold farmers" who undertake dreary, repetitive labor to produce virtual wealth that's sold to players with more money and less patience than them. The structural differences between in-game play and in-game work are mostly arbitrary, and "real" work is half a game, anyway. Most of the people you see going to work today are LARPing (live-action role playing) an incredibly boring RPG (role-playing game) called "professionalism" that requires them to alter their vocabulary, posture, eating habits, facial expressions—every detail all the way down to what they allow themselves to find funny.

The most amazing thing about the moment we're living through is the degree to which it allows us to abolish all the boring stuff that used to be required for any kind of ambitious project. We're at a point where we can build an encyclopedia with the kind of organizational structures that were once only good enough to run an ambitious fun fair or bake sale. Hierarchy and injustice are far from dead, but the justification for continuing them gets weaker with every passing moment.

The net doesn't solve the problem of injustice, but it solves the first hard problem of righting wrongs: getting everyone together and keeping them together. You still have to do the even harder work of risking life, limb, personal fortune, and reputation.

Every wonderful thing in our world has a fight in its history: our rights, our good fortune, our happiness. All that is sweet was paid for, once upon a time, by principled people who risked everything to change the world for the better.

Those risks are not diminished one iota by the net. But the rewards are every bit as sweet.

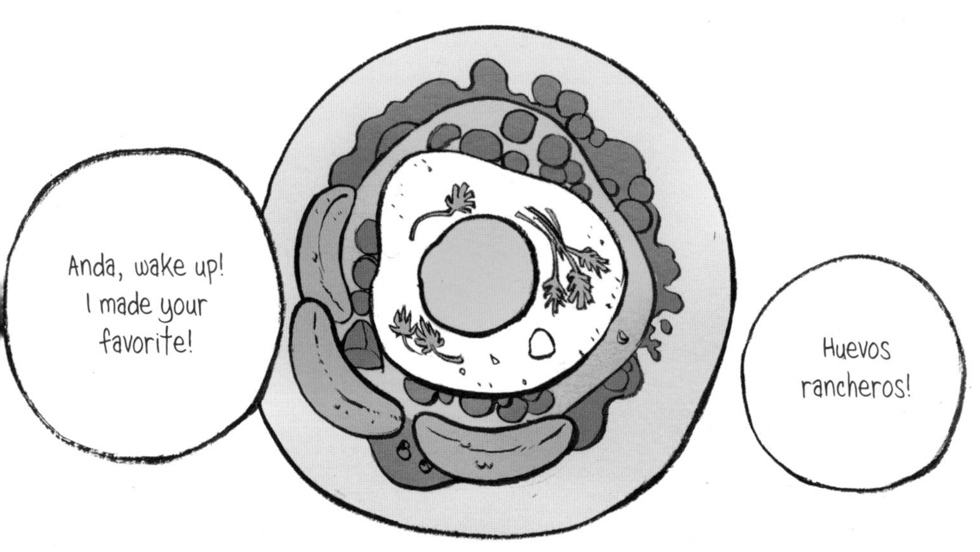
Anda, wake up! I made your favorite!
Huevos rancheros!

Happy birthday, sweetpea!

Thanks, Mom.
Oaties
Happy birthday, Anda.
Bye, Dad.
I have something for you.

Oh, heeey. Phil's!
Phil's BBQ
SAN ☆ DIEGO
Thought you must miss that place. It's got a postcard from Grandma, too!
Happy Birthday!
Hope you're adjusting to your new home. Here're some gifts from home. Miss you!
♡ Grandma
Anda Bridge
1327 6th Ave.
Flagstaff, AZ 86004
Thanks, Mom.

Honey, look out the window!

TURKEY TROT SIGN UPS
THURSDAY 11/15th!!
Happy Birthday!
you're adjusting
your new home. Here're
fts from home.
Miss you!
♡ Grandma
Ando Bridge
1327 6th Ave.
Flagstaff, AZ 86004

myprograms-bash-59
mmhs201 : myprograms andabridge python
there are 10 things
Adding: grass
there are 11 things
Adding : bee

Class! Listen up! We have a guest speaker today! Miss Liza McCombs comes all the way from Australia.
I hope you give her your full attention. Miss McCombs?
Thank you, Miss Bronson. Hullo, class!
Call me Liza the Organiza.

I'm a gamer and I kick arse. No, seriously.
I organize a guild online and I'm looking for a few of you chickens to join me.
GAME OVER

This is Coarsegold Online, the fastest growing massive multiplayer role-playing game . . .

. . . with over 10 million subscribers world-wide. You might've heard of it.

See, that's a tragedy. Practically makes me weep.
When I started gaming online there were no women gamers. I was one of the best gamers in the world and I couldn't even be proud of who I was.

It's different now, but it's still not perfect. We're going to change that, chickens, you lot and me.
Here's my offer to the ladies:
if you will play as a girl in Coarsegold Online, you will be given probationary memberships in the Clan Fahrenheit. If you measure up in three months, you'll be full-fledged members.

Who's in, ladies? Who wants to be a girl in-game and out?

Coarsegold
online
TEEN
T
ESRB
OVER
10 MILLION
SUBSCRIBERS
WORLDWIDE!

Hey Mom? Would it be okay if I subscribe to an online game?
I need a credit card to sign up.

Online?
It's only $12 a month and I'll pay for it. I'll get some babysitting gigs, this is just upfront.

What's wrong with your offline games?

A speaker came to my class today and said it would boost my self-esteem to play with a guild. It's like a team sport.

But that means you chat with strangers?
Yes, but the guild I'm playing for is all girls and invite-only. See, it's even rated T for Teen.

I dunno, dear. I just don't think it's safe. You know that's where perverts go to meet kids.

Not interested in any of that, Mom. Please? For my birthday?

You only talk to other girls your age, you hear?
Only girls! Thanks, Mom!

USERNAME

PASSWORD

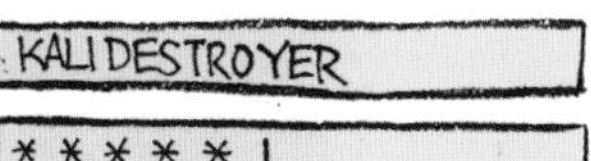

LOADING

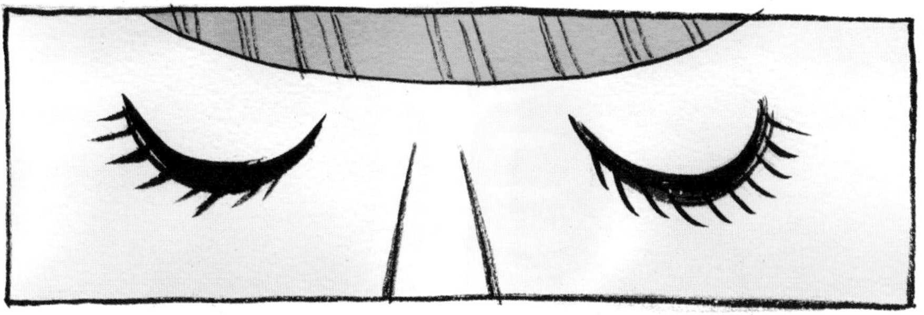

RACE

HUMAN
UNDEAD
PIXIE
PLANTON
BEAST

CLASS

SCHOLAR
WARRIOR
HUNTER
THIEF
HEALER
PRIEST

HAIR

DRESS

♀ KALIDESTROYER

STORE
WEAPONS
BROADSWORD
SABER
DAGGER
PONIARD
RAPIER
BLUTO'S DAGGER
BATTLE AXE
SPIKED FLAIL
CHAIN
BACK
NEXT
NOW ENTERING COARSEGOLD...
LEVEL 1

NEEDED

warriors
and alchemists
for raid in
Scholar City

HAIRY
LONGPO TUSK
+15 GOLD

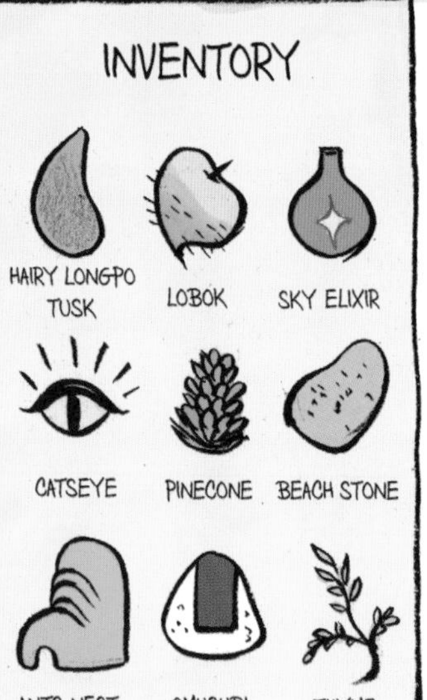
INVENTORY
HAIRY LONGPO TUSK
LOBOK
SKY ELIXIR
CATSEYE
PINECONE
BEACH STONE
ANTS NEST
OMUSUBI
THYME

LEVEL
2

Nice WORK, recruit.
Thanks, Sarge.

Haven't seen anyone slay undead like that since I was a probationary member.
I like you, Anda. You're like me, you're bloodthirsty.

Thanks. That means a lot.
Spare me the fan-girling.

What time zone are you at? I wanna make sure there are no problems with bed-times, dinners, and all that.
I'm in New York, Eastern Standard Time.
I'm in Flagstaff.
What?

Where the hell is Flagstaff?
Arizona, I'm on Mountain Time.

Oh and we don't observe Daylight Saving Time.
Weird.

So you want to try something different, Small Town? What do you think about making some cash?

Cash? You mean gold?

When I said cash I meant cash.

. . .

Sigh.
Can you go voice?

Hello?
I'm here! Hello? Lucy?

Call me Sarge! Look, I have a mission that pays real cash. Whichever PayPal you're using, they'll deposit money into it. Looks fun, too.

That's a bit weird, Sarge. Is that against Clan rules?

What? No, geez. All the executives in the Clan pay rent doing missions for money. Some of them are even rich from it! You can make a lot of money gaming, you know.

It's not—you know—pervy, is it?

Gag me. No. Geez, Anda. Are you nuts? They just want us to go kill some guys.
Okay, we're good at that.

Excellent! Now come on, it's over at the Plantation.
Wait, where're you going?
Gettin' a ride.
100
STORK
I can afford it.

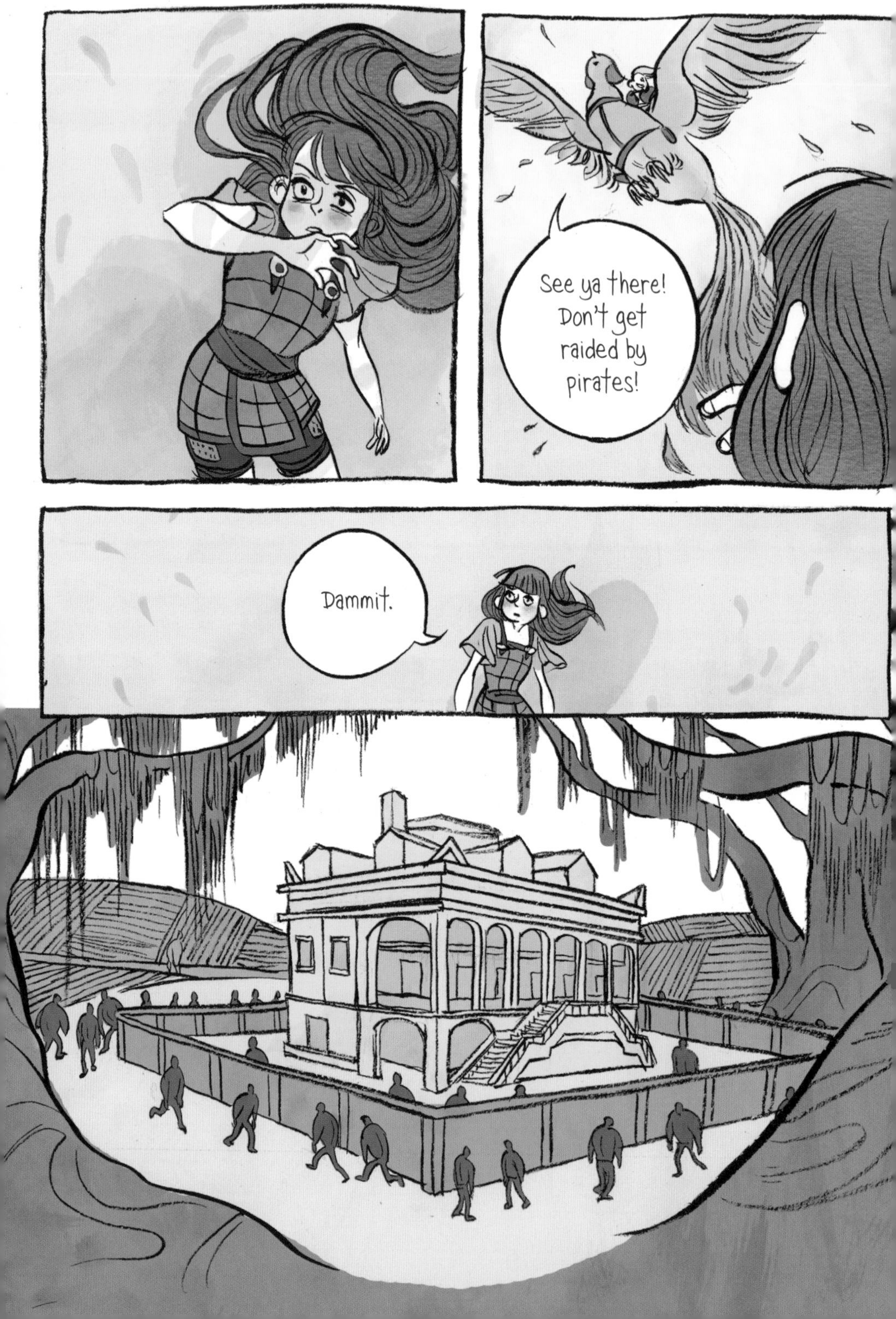

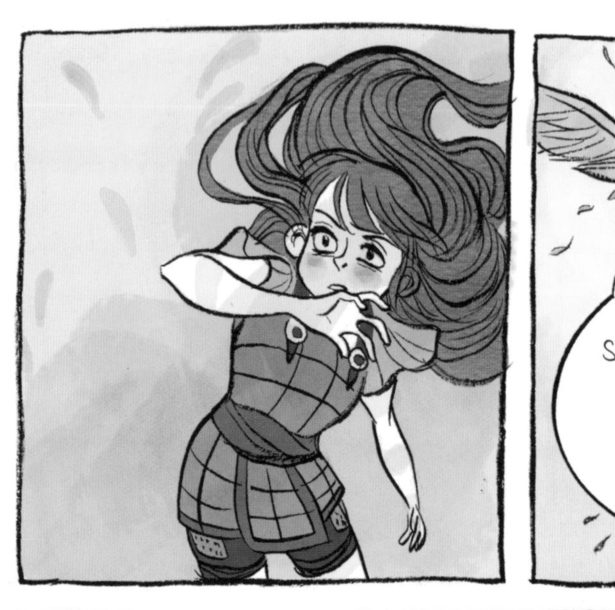

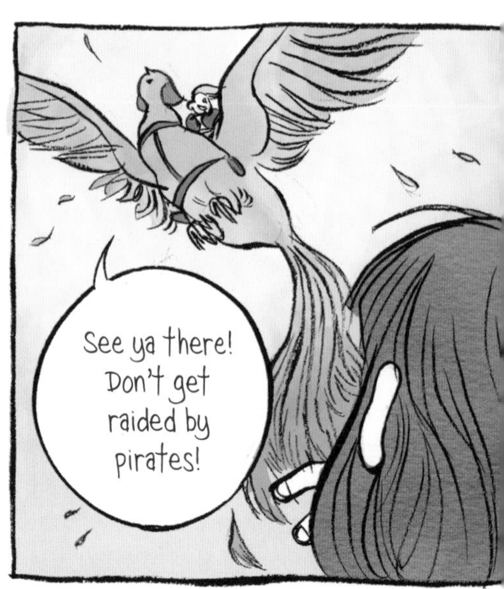

See ya there! Don't get raided by pirates!

Dammit.

You made it! Wow, leveled up and everything now. Look, that's the house we want to raid.
Stand back, I'm gonna use the BFG.

WEAPONS
GUNS

Yee haw!! That was TOO easy.
Okay, we gotta move fast.
They'll be expecting us. Ready?
Um—
Go, go, go!!

BATTLE
AXE

10
Ah!
21
14
17%
5
10%

32
4
45
Got 'im!
Lucy! Behind you!

Lucy!

Call me Sarge!!
I'm all the way at the Infirmary, Anda! Bloody hell, it'll take me 10 minutes to resurrect!
I can complete the mission, Sarge. Just tell me what to do.
You sure? Enter the cottage and kill all the gold farmers.
The what?
Gold farmers. All the people inside!
Okay.
And Anda? This is important. Don't blow it.
I won't.

Are you players or bots?

Are you "gold farmers"?

Lucy, they're not fighting back.

Good. Kill 'em all.
Really?
Yeah—that's the orders. Kill 'em all and then haul ass back to the City Center.
Okay.

等一下！
請不要...
15
LEVEL 4

Hahahaha!

Did you . . . get a job recently or something?
Actually I've been playing Coarsegold and—
Hey! You're the Sci-Fi Club, right?
Prep alert, prep alert.
Are you guys playing D&D?
Um, yes.
That's so cool! You know, I'm trying to start a board game club. I think you guys would be perfect.
What kind of board games?

Oh, you know, like, Scrabble and Jenga.

Pictionary, Bananagrams . . .

I think you have the wrong idea. Those games you mentioned? Everyone knows how to play. I'm not sure you really need us.

But that's the point! I want all kinds of people to join. You could be, like, the "Ambassadors of D&D."

D&D and Jenga are, like, completely different things.

So thanks, but I think we're cool just playing here.

Okay, well. Let me know if you change your minds.

What a tool.

So what were you saying, Anda?
Huh?
'Bout Coarsegold?

Oh, yeah. I've been doing paid missions. I didn't know you could do that before.

Really, they pay you? For what?
To clean up bots, I think.

So you're, like, a virtual soldier?
Like fight spam? That's pretty productive.
Yeah!

Yeah, exactly.

COARSEGOLD
ONLINE
KALIDESTROYER
*****|
ENTER

Okay, lemme get this right. Mexican.
Bot.
Japanese.
Not bot.
Korean.
Not bot.
<planton rug> $550
<whip> $100
<ninja stars> $70
<maglar juice> $90

Chinese.
SUPER bot. Look, it's not hard. Just talk to them, and if they don't respond or speak English you should probably kill 'em.

Sorry, it's just a little confusing.

Here, lemme show you something.

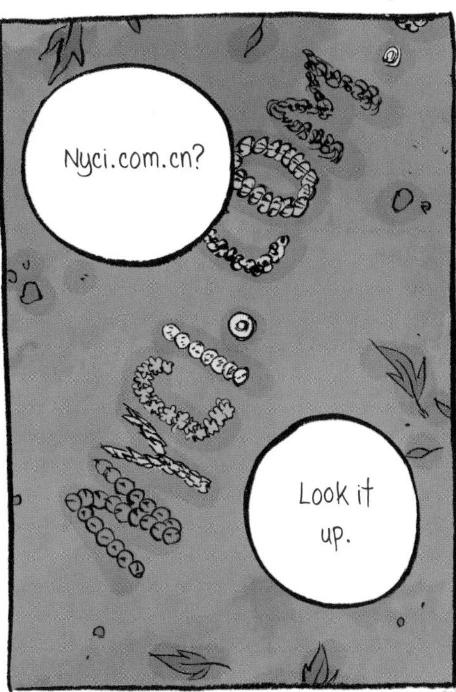

NYCI·COM·CN

ID	LEVEL	RACE/CLASS	PRICE (USD)	
CO Account 000325	90	BEAST/SCHOLAR	$356.00	BUY
CO Account 000326	90	UNDEAD/PRIEST	$399.00	BUY
CO Account 000327	90	HUMAN / HUNTER	$180.00	BUY
CO Account 000328	90	/ THIEF	$210.00	BUY
CO Account 000329		/ PRIEST	$167.00	BUY
CO Acco 330		THIEF	$499.00	BUY

They're selling . . .

gold?

Look! Over there.

Look at them, greedy assholes.
What are they doing?

They're FARMING.
They collect items for gold and sell the gold to other players for cash.
Isn't that against the rules?
Like they care.
Oh my god! You can buy a level 85 avatar for $100! And a house! You can buy a whole furnished house for $600!
People spend MONTHS trying to earn that much gold. How is this fair?
3 BEDROOM BOATHOUSE

Exactly. Makes me sick.
I've spent my whole life proving...

I'm as good a gamer as any other dude... and I had to do it without cheats.
But these crappy players can buy a house on Day 1. It isn't fair.

So this is what we're getting paid to do. Kill gold farmers. By who?

Other gold farmers, okay?

You have a problem with it?

Some dudes who're jealous the other guy is snatching all the good territory. I'm playing them both.

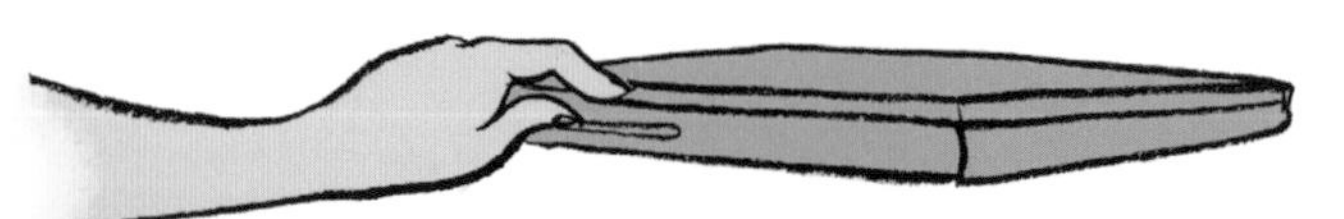

No. I'm with you. Let's wipe these gold farmers out.

Here, take this. It'll give you a boost.

You spent 90 gold on this??

90 gold is nothing when you're the baddest bitch in the virtual universe.

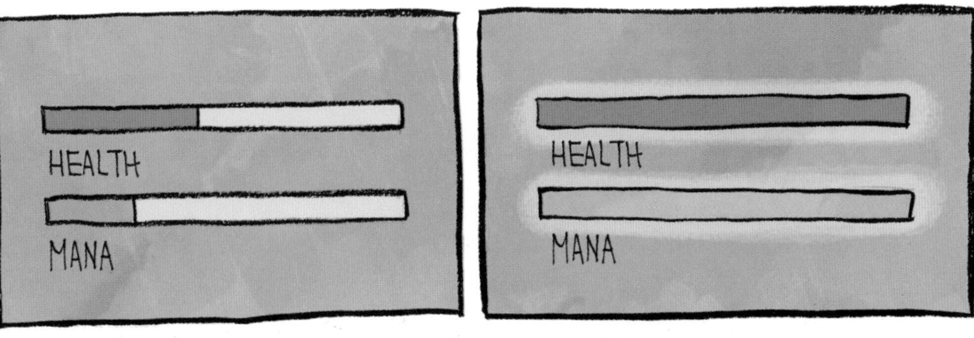
HEALTH
MANA
HEALTH
MANA

Don't let them get away! When they die they drop all their gold!

Where are you going?
That one hit me!

There's no way out, gold farmer!
Let's just get it over with!
Shhh!

The Emerald Macaw!
THE Emerald Macaw
• RACE : BEAST
• LEVEL 14
• FREQUENCY: RARE
• EMERALD FEATHERS WORTH 450 GOLD

EMERALD FEATHER
+450 GOLD

That was amazing. Where'd you learn to do that?

Play.
Do you speak English?
Little. I play Coarsegold.

What were you doing with those gold farmers?

Your English isn't good enough . . .

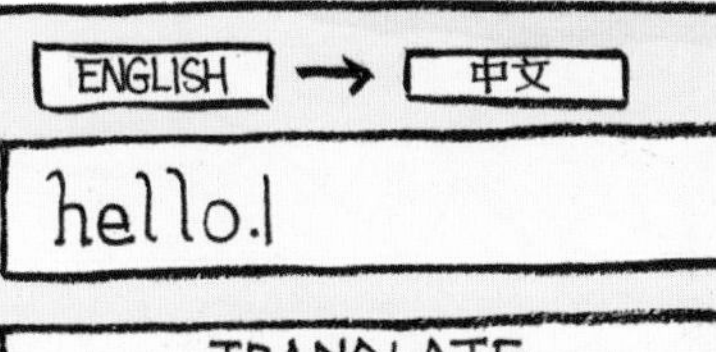
ENGLISH → 中文
hello.|
TRANSLATE

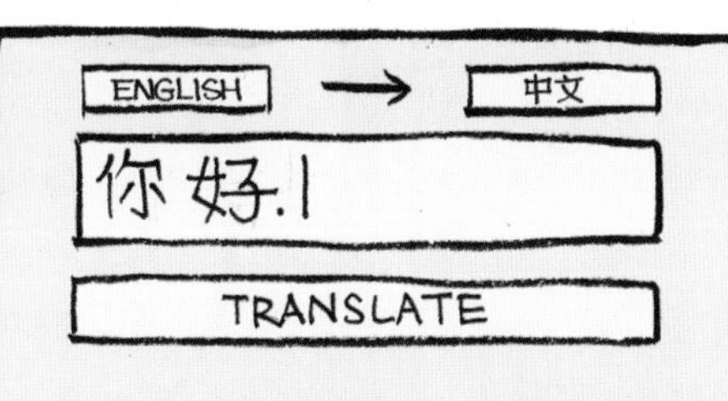
ENGLISH → 中文
你好.|
TRANSLATE

(hello)

(Whoa, you know Chinese?)

(I can with Translator. What you were doing with all those gold farmers?
I almost killed you!)

(I am a gold farmer. That is my job.)

(It's what I do for money.
But I'm on my break right now, which is why I'm—)

Got him! All right!
Second completed mission of the day! Sorry about the runner.

Normally they just stand there while you hack 'em to death.
Let's head back to base and buy more weapons.
I wanna get something with a better range.
1
SUN TEMPLE
7AM CST

WORLD CLOCK
FLAGSTAFF, ARIZONA
SHENZHEN, CHINA
MOUNTAIN TIME
CHINA STANDARD TIME

gold farming

Web
Images
Videos
News
More

Talk to me in English.

What?
Talk to me in English! So I can learn.

Hello! My name is Anda.

My name is Raymond. I live in China.

Raymond's an English name.

Raymond is my name in English class.

You're a student? How old are you?

(How else am I going to play?)

(I'm a gamer. I collect gold for work but on my own time I play Coarsegold like you. Right now I have free time because my shift ended at 6 AM.)

Ended at 6 AM??
(I work the night shift. I like it better when it's dark and the boss is asleep.)

So why did you contact me? I tried to kill you.

(You're the first non-gold farmer who's tried to talk to me.)

It's not personal. I know it's just your job, but we want things to be fair.

Gold farming messes with the value of gold.

(I don't care about that. I just want to join a guild and play with real gamers. Even with a different avatar, everyone is suspicious of the guy who only speaks Chinese.)

Well, you can't join my guild.

On top of the gold farmer thing, we don't allow boys.

Can you show me how you cast that spell yesterday?

How did you get so good at this, Raymond?

(I play Coarsegold 16 hours a day. 12 for work, 4 for myself.)

Wow. But you're like my age. How're you allowed to work so much?
(I lied and told them I was 18.)

18??

(My family doesn't have enough money to send me to college, so why not? If I'm not working I'm just wasting time.)

But what do your parents think?

(They don't know. They know I work but they don't consider this a real job.
They'd rather I work in a factory making zippers instead of doing something I enjoy.)

At least you're around other people who are like you.
(Maybe. It can be hard to make friends in a new city.)
I know what you mean.
(Anyway, I should get going. My back is hurting.)
Hahaha, what an old man.
(No, seriously. I was lifting boxes at a factory before this. It gets especially bad when I've been sitting too long.)
(Sometimes I have to excuse myself to the bathroom so I can lie on the floor a little while.)

That sounds awful! Why aren't you going to the doctor?
(I can't go to any local doctors!)
(I'm registered as a resident of Hunan, so I can only go to the doctor back home.)
(I'm worried if I go home I'll never come back.)
But if you keep this up you might not be able to work at all.
(It's okay, my friend Ah Duo is good with his hands. I've been trading him cigarettes for massages, and it helps.)

This isn't right.
What about your boss? Can't you get your job to cover the costs?

(I don't know. I'm not sure how that works . . .)

(I have to go. It's the other guy's turn to use the computer.)

Wait!

(You don't have to do anything.)
I'm going to figure out a way to help you. You're going to feel better.
I want to. As a Fahrenheit, it is my duty to protect.

Okay. Where can I meet you again?

(I don't know where I'm going to be tomorrow but I'll let you know. It'll be the same time.)

Okay.

(We have to move around every day so people don't know where to find us.)

Z
Z
Z

Anda,
sit down.

Who is Ross Winterland?
Who?
And Damon Carmichael, and Adrien Weiver.
I don't know who you're talking about!
Who are these people depositing
money in your PayPal account?
Account Statement | November
Bridge, Anda
Email (PayPal Account ID):
Account Activity
Date
11/18/2013
11/20/2013
11/22/2013
/2013
Description
Payment from Ross Winterland
Payment from Damon Carmichael
Payment from Ross Winterland
Payment from Adrien Weiver
Amount
$20.00
$20.00
$20.00
$20.00
TOTAL BALANCE $80.00

Oh my god.

In case you've forgotten, sweetie, that's my bank account you're wired to. Tell me. WHY are strangers sending you money?

Mom, this isn't what you think! They're just paying me for missions within the game. I'm serious. That's ALL there is. That's why I didn't tell you, I didn't think it was important.

I told you not to talk to strange men on the Internet.
But I've never talked to these people in my life! I don't even know who they are!

But you're okay with accepting their money? You realize how hard this makes it for me to trust you?
I knew this was a bad idea. Starting now, no more online games.
Mom!!
In fact . . .
. . . no recreational Internet use for a week. I'm sorry but you have to learn this is not okay.

Mom, listen, there's a gamer in China—
China!

He's stuck in a factory and he's sick. I told him I'd help him . . .
Would you listen to yourself! Absolutely not! You're not speaking to any of these people ever again!

Mom, you're overreacting! You're just afraid of things you don't understand!

I understand the world can be a cruel place and there are people out there counting on naive kids like you to take advantage of.
Don't just think because it's video games people can't get hurt.

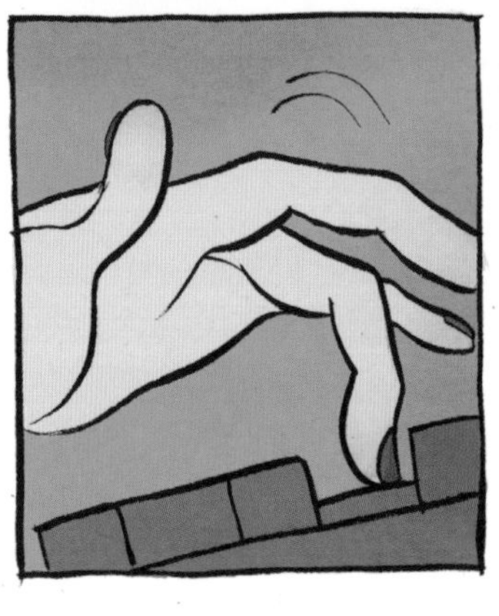

YOU ARE NOT CONNECTED
TO THE INTERNET

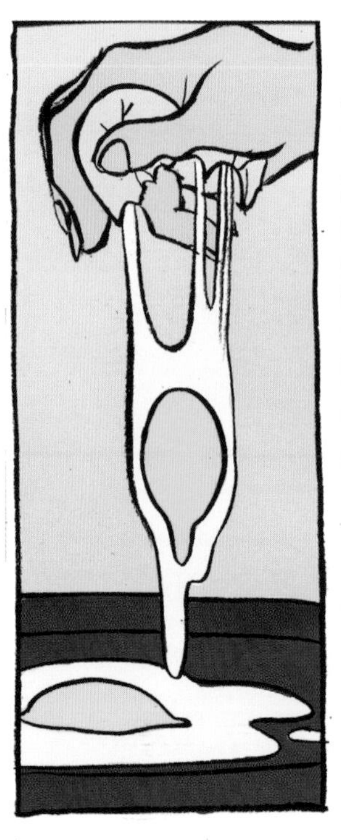

with American cheese and two thick juicy slices of bacon

don't let tha
get

phhhbbbbbt
bbbt phbbbt

Uh! Hey! Ooh Ooh, Girl!

Anda, can you turn that down a little.
29
Since Saturday, December 8 at noon, Goodman Manufacturing, which employs more than 1,000 people, has been on strike.
Gorsh Mowee, I can't wait for the Pwincess's Pwahty!

Wait, no, no, go back, turn it up!
Gimme the remote.

—will be held next Monday.
WORKERS STRIKE

The new offer from the company is expected to be accepted.
WORKERS STRIKE

Workers say it's especially difficult because of the Christmas holiday. Nobody wants to disappoint their family, especially the children.

Despite the pressure to reach an agreement by the holidays, both workers and management alike remain confident.

Differences between the proposals involve wages and employer contributions to medical coverage. The vote is expected to take place next Monday.

I'm Sarah Tanaka, Channel 2 News.

Hey, Anda, you joining us?

What's up? Making a new game?

Research.

Café
PC BANG
PC CAFE
OPEN
•INTERNET
•GAMES
•PC/MAC

BANG
TIME IN
TIME OUT
OM
3:15
BEN
3:32
Sam
3:45
ANDA

[Message translated in Chinese: I'm back. Where do I meet you?]

我回來了。我在哪裡見到你？

LUCY 12/5
LUCY 12/5
LUCY 12/5
LUCY 12/6
LUCY 12/6
LUCY 12/7

Anda! Jesus, where've you been? It's been two weeks!
Lucy—I mean, Sarge. Sorry, my Internet's out. I'm actually at a cafe.
All right, well gimme a little heads up next time.
Check it out, I got some new recruits!
Recruits, Anda.
Anda, recruits.

AAAAAHHHHH!!
We've heard so much about you!
Come hunt with us?
Anda!
Lucy says you're, like, unforgivingly good at killing gold farmers.
Hah. Yeah. Um. Actually, Lucy, I wanted to talk to you about that.
The gold-farming thing.

I think . . .

Help me.
I think Liza pulled these noobs from some middle school afterschool program.
They've never played a non-cell phone game in their life.
Hey Sergeant?

How do I, um, get unstuck?
Just hold on!

Please. Don't make me do this alone.
I'd really love to help, Lucy, but I . . .

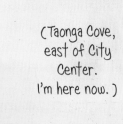

(Taonga Cove, east of City Center. I'm here now.)

Sorry, I gotta go! I'll see you tomorrow!
It ain't dinnertime, you liar!
Daylight Saving!
TAONGA COVE

I'm so glad I could catch you. Sorry I haven't been online.

Me too.

Let's go someplace a little more private.

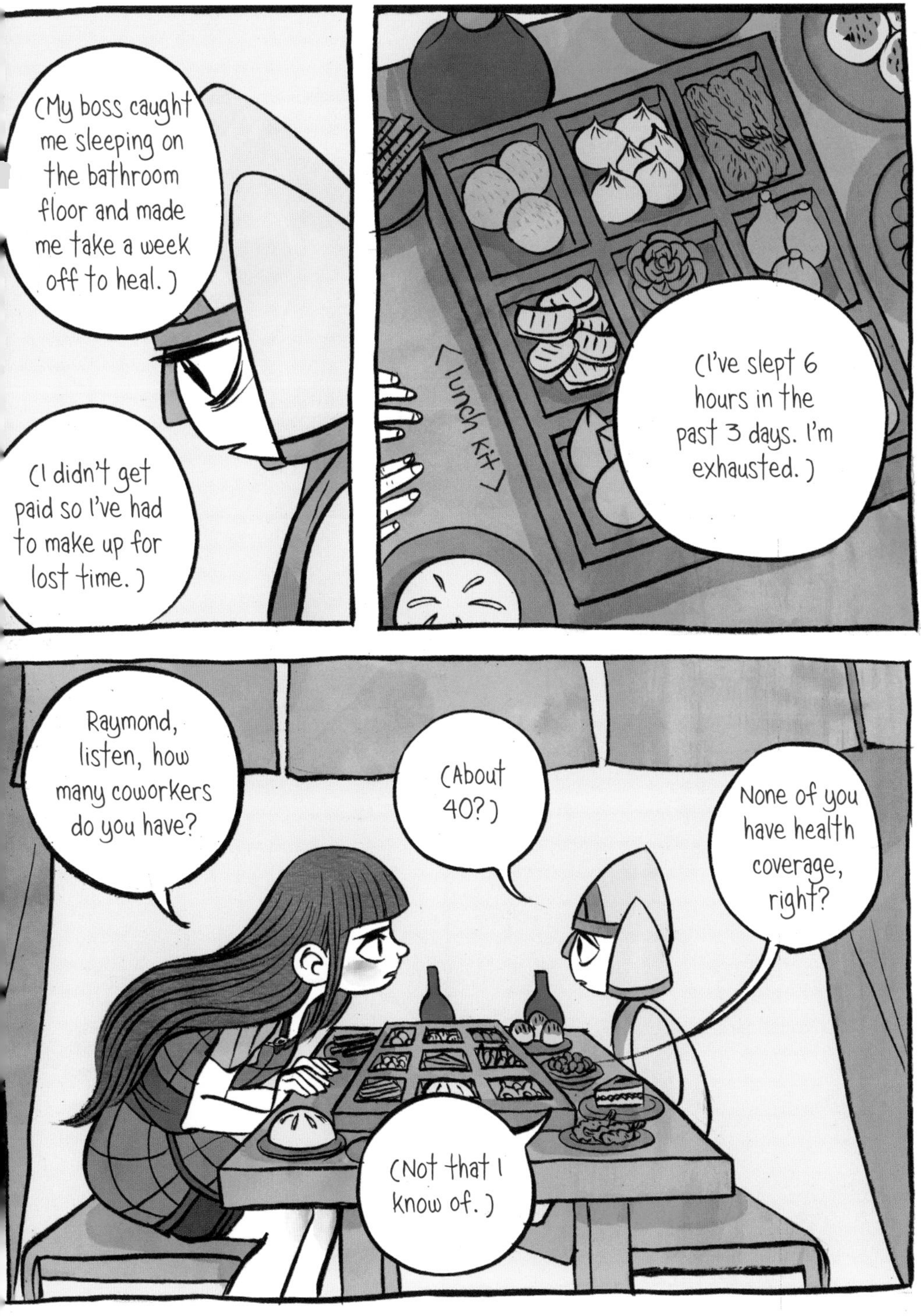

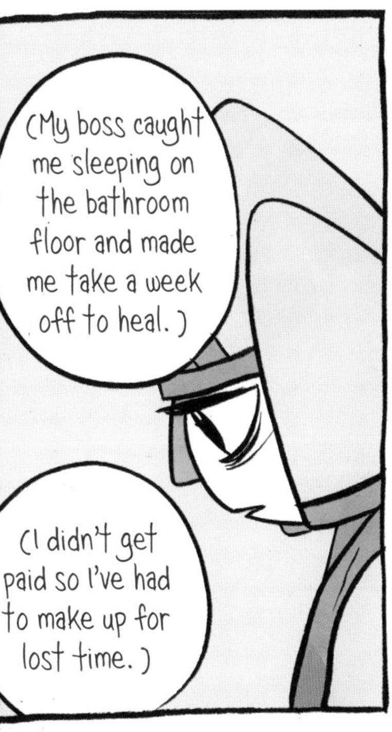
(My boss caught me sleeping on the bathroom floor and made me take a week off to heal.)
(I didn't get paid so I've had to make up for lost time.)

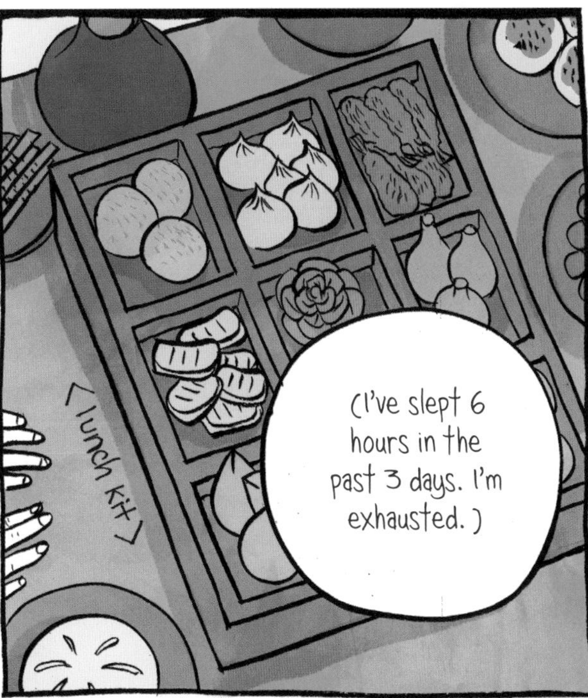
<lunch kit>
(I've slept 6 hours in the past 3 days. I'm exhausted.)

Raymond, listen, how many coworkers do you have?
(About 40?)
None of you have health coverage, right?
(Not that I know of.)

Go to your coworkers. Tell everyone you need to demand health care together.
I looked it up, there's a Urban Resident Basic Medical Insurance that you're all eligible for. As long as you work in the city, you can go to the doctor!
(What if our boss says no?)
You go on a strike. My dad's company is going through this right now.
If you walk out together, you'll have power on your side.
(But what if my coworkers aren't interested? We're all young and I'm the only one who's sick.)

That's why you're so important. You're a living example of why things need to change.

If you're keeping your problems a secret, so might somebody else!

(But I've never done anything like this before. I'm so inexperienced.)

Don't worry, I'll help. I'm gonna talk to my dad and get some advice.
We'll work out the details. The important thing is you start spreading the word.

(Okay. God, I think I'm gonna be sick.)
Good. You'll need health insurance!

(Haha. Thanks, Anda.)

Let's do it. I'll do my homework, you do yours, and let's meet again tomorrow, okay?

SLEEP

EXIT

Z Z Z Z

ZZzz
ZZzz

So a sit-down strike is when people go to work as usual but don't do any work?
Right, so if their bosses hire other people to work during the strike, the sit down prevents that.
GALA FO
Hmm, that's really smart. That's basically what protesters do, right?
It is. And since when were you so interested in what your dad does?
Well, it affects me too. What happens if the strike takes place and it doesn't work?

I don't think it'll come to that. And I wouldn't worry about how this affects you. It won't.

Your life is secure here. I make sure of that.

I know, Dad. Believe me. I feel very lucky.

CRAZY
COLORZ

Oh h-hey,
Anda.
Hey
guys!

INBOX EMPTY
Hmmm.

Guess I'll go wait at my house.

Raymond, I'm here! Why didn't you message me?

I talked to my dad yesterday and got some tips from him.
I think you can do it! Raymond?

Raymond?

你買嗎？

I knew it.

Lucy!

I knew you've been meeting a gold farmer. Why??
Lucy, I can explain. This one is different. Raymond's a real gamer! Gold farming is just a job.
What are you talking about? He's a GOLD FARMER. What part of that do you not understand?
What else is he supposed to do?
Make zippers for 25 cents a day?
What about the part where we made money killing gold farmers?

We were exploiting the game too!
Oh screw you! That was totally different and you know it.
Nothing I've done has EVER been about money.
Yeah, because it's been all about you! The "Sergeant" thing?
The giant showy fortress? The only reason gold farming bothers you is because you can't stand other people getting ahead!
You're a bully!

A bully, huh?
Lucy, I'm sorry . . .
I'll show YOU a bully.
Danisa! Finish him!

Lucy,
don't!

Lucy, I'm
telling you,
stop!!

YAHHHHHHH!!
You BITCH.
You killed my cat!!

HYAA HH!!
ATTACKS
BLACK ARROW
FIREBALL
CALL PET
BEAR TRAP
CAMOUFLAGE
ATTACKS
BLOODBATH
SMASH
RAGE THROW
SHIELD
TAUNT

10%

0%

(Raymond!)
(Why won't you listen to me!)
(So it's you? You're the American he was talking about?)
(Raymond doesn't work here anymore.)
(The boss caught him conspiring to take down the company and fired him immediately. It was your idea, wasn't it?)
I. . . .

(Nice job, American. You don't know anything about us.
Next time stick to your own game.)

From: LIZA <liza@lizanator.com>
To: Anda

Anda,

I heard about your incident with Lucy yesterday. I've also been informed of the two of you dabbling in paid anti gold-farming missions. I wouldn't normally care what you do on your own time except you are representing the Fahrenheits, and harassing others is against our mission. You are both temporarily suspended until I've decided on a suitable punishment.

Yours,
Liza

Anda, come here! Let's get a photo!

FOUNTAIN

Triple scoop sundae, please.

Oh honey, you're on a diet, that's too much!

Can we change that to single scoop? Thanks.
Oh come on, we're celebrating here!

Just because you have better health coverage now doesn't mean you're allowed to blow it.
I'm not blowing anything! Anda, what would you like?
I don't want any.

You don't want—?
Tsk, see what you've done, you've scared
daughter off.

Well, good for her.
Sweetheart, don't listen to your mother, ice cream won't kill you.
I said I don't want any.
It won't kill you, but it'll make your butt bigger!
Jesus Christ, what's wrong with you, it's JUST ICE CREAM!!
At least if I get fat and fall over I'll have enough health insurance to suck all the ice cream outta me!
Not everyone does!

Anda? Are you feeling better?
What's bothering you?
I'm sorry I yelled at you. Everything's just been so stressful lately.
Is it because I banned your video games?

No. It's because you're right. The world is a cruel place. Especially in video games.
Oh, my sweetheart . . .
Come on. Come watch TV with me.
There's still some dinner left over.

NEW MESSAGE
onebadclam:
Do you have a minute?
andapanda: Who is this?
onebadclam: Lucy.
Can I talk to you over video chat?

andapanda: one sec

ACCEPT

DANISA

Hey.
Hey, Sarge.

You don't have to call me that now. I'm suspended, remember?

Why am I even here . . .

You probably think I'm here to yell at you. Well, I'm not. This morning before I got kicked off, this noob found me. He wouldn't leave me alone, kept calling your name, so I assumed he was looking for you.

He said his name was "Ah Duo" and he wanted to send you something.

He seemed pretty upset.

He's being made an example of. Oh, Raymond.

It's all my fault.

He was near Pirate Island farming for dog furs.

I don't know if he's still there but you might be able to catch him if you hurry.

What am I going to say to him?

Raymond's your friend, right? Maybe you both want to clear his name.

Thank you, Lucy. And Lucy?

You're not a bully. You're a fighter. Anyone would be lucky to be your recruit.

Get outta here, fangirl.

PC BAANG
• INTERNET
GAMES

KALIDESTROYER
*****1
ENTER

USER: BLOCKED

Dammit!
aevaegaegahl
CREATE AVATAR

No.
No, no, no, NO!
NO!
I don't have TIME to level up!
BZZZT
INBOX
FROM: LUCY
Thought you might need some reinforcements. Here's the roster of recruits.
MILA - milaloft@gmail.com
KARINE - karineanne94@gmail.
JANEY - janebrain@yahoo.
SAEWON - saewonkim@gm
PRU - phirsch@gmail.com
BEATRICE - elderbea@gmail.com
CAROLINE - carolee4@gmail.com
ALINNA - alinnahsu@yahoo.com
LYLA - leeleekitty@gmail.com
STELLA - smella92@yahoo.com
STAR - starryconnor@gmail.com
LYNN - lsrodriguez@comcast.net

Ladies! So glad to see you. I need an escort to Pirate Island.

Anything for a friend of the Sarge!

Why are you a noob all of a sudden?

It's hard to explain.
It's okay, we trust you.
Are we ready for this, Fahrenheits?
Um, are you ready for this?
Let's go to Pirate Island!

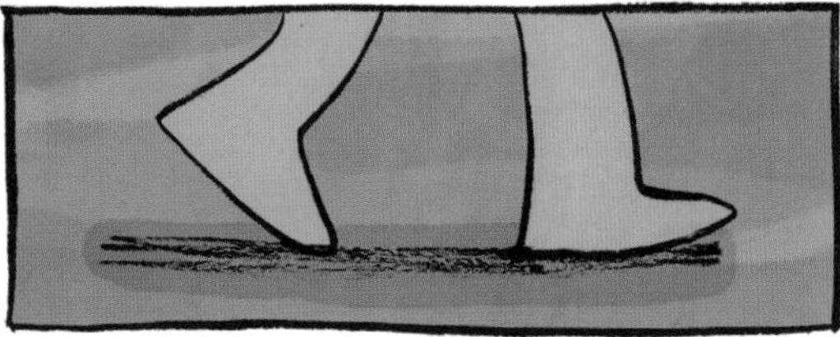

(Are any of you Ah Duo?)
(I'm Anda. Raymond's friend—)
(I know who you are.)
(Please leave us alone.)
(Wait, hear me out. Please!)

(Please! I'm really sorry what happened to Raymond.)

(I thought if I was his friend—)

(It was my fault. I made him believe things would be okay.)

(No, I was his friend.)

(I looked out for him. Raymond's a kid. He played here, slept here, and ate here. This was his whole world it's gone.)

(You think just because you can read about us on the Internet you know everything about us.)

(I know, you are absolutely right.)
(I don't know what it's like to live in China . . .)
(and I don't know what it's like to be a gold farmer.)
(But I do know what it's like to be a kid who loves video games.)
(If you would give me a chance, I will do anything to help you get him back.)

(If you really care about him, you will help me spread his message.)
(It's a call to action. I can't let my coworkers know it's from me.)
我是NYCI的员工.
我是负责玩 Coarsegold 的.
我愿意继续玩下去.
但是我的身体状
不允许我这麽作, 然而,
让我去作治疗几乎是不可能的.
因为NYCI认为治病是我个人的事.
但是NYCI不知道, 不照顾
员工对NYCI其实是有害的.
一旦有不幸的事情 发生在所
有员工身上时, 难到所有员工
也得自己负责吗?
如今, 会发生在我身上的问题,
难到不会发生在你身上吗?
因此, 请加入这抗争的行列.
我一个人的抗争是无效的,
但集众人的力量 是可以成事的.
-张唤义
(Things are already tense because of what happened to Raymond.)
(If you tell me where your coworkers are, I can have the Fahrenheits send this to them.)

I have a mission for you.

Copy and paste this into your message box.
我是NYCI的员工.
我是负责玩 Coarsegold 的.
我愿意继续玩下去.
但是我的身体状
不允许我这麼作, 然而,
让我去作治疗几乎是不可能的.
因为NYCI认为治病是我个人的事.
但是NYCI不知道, 不照顾
员工对NYCI其实是有害的.
一旦有不幸的事情 发生在所
有员工身上时, 难到所有员工
也得自己负责
如今, 会发生在
难到不会发
因此, 请加
我一个
但集众人
Canvass these areas for all avatars that respond to "Nyci.com.cn" and send this to them.

What does it say?

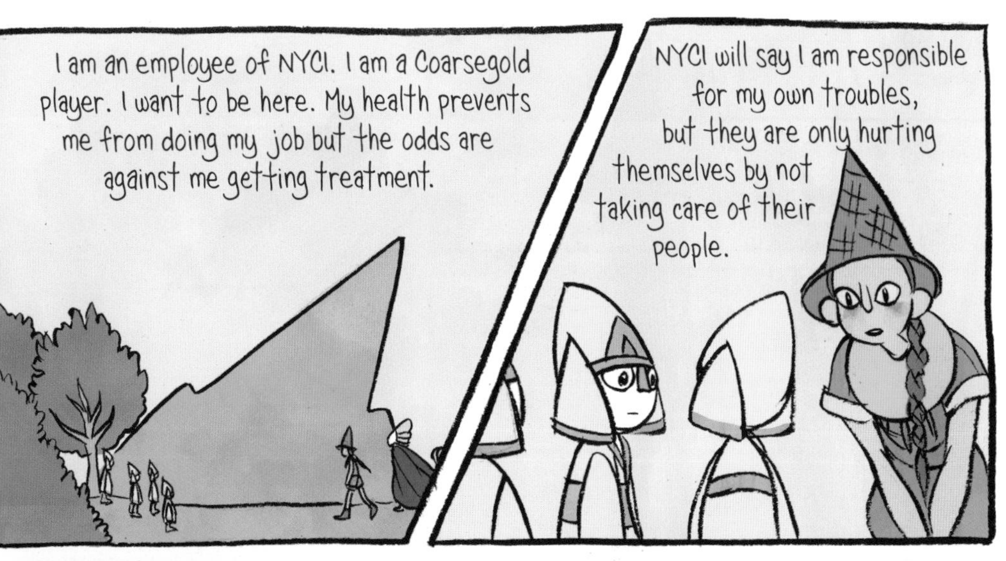
I am an employee of NYCI. I am a Coarsegold player. I want to be here. My health prevents me from doing my job but the odds are against me getting treatment.
NYCI will say I am responsible for my own troubles, but they are only hurting themselves by not taking care of their people.

What if misfortune were to befall us all? If it happened to me, couldn't it happen to any of us? Please join me in my fight.

(Well, I'm going to do something.)

張喚義
XX公司
(We have some demands.)

WELCO
PARENT

You move when the magician moves his hand.
Oh, Anda. I'm amazed at you! I had no idea you could do this.
Dammit!
Thanks, Mom.
WELCOME PARENTS

Hello, Anda! Great to see you again.
You must be Anda's parents. I'm Liza, I organize the guild your daughter plays in.
Oh! Nice to meet you, Liza. Can't say I know a lot about what you do, but it's nice to know there's an adult out there.
Yes. I'm sure you already know this but your daughter is an amazingly mature young woman.
I had suspended her recently due to suspected bullying . . .
But turns out she was doing the opposite. She was standing up for bullied players.
It took a lot of courage.

Anyway, I would like to formally reinvite Anda back into the guild, if she'd like. Officially as a member this time. She'd be great for the new recruits we have.
Actually, my parents . . .
She would love to.
Mom?
I think it's good she's taking on new responsibilities. I trust her.
Yes. I'd love to.

Oh hey, Steph!

Are you still trying to put together a board game club?

Yeah.

I'd love to help out.

Really? You would?
Yeah. And actually, you should join us for D&D sometime.
I'll talk to the guys. It'll be like research.

Oh, that would be so awesome! Thank you!

Today you join ranks with some of the finest players in Coarsegold!
You will play honorably, you will play fiercely, and above all, you will show others what it takes to be extraordinary.

It is not gender, nor age, nor race, but your ability to work hard at what you love.
Today, you become leaders.
Today, you become Fahrenheits!

Thanks for vouching for me, Small Town.
Couldn't have done it without you, Sarge.

Care to
dance?

Why not?
This palace so beautiful. Some day I like have something beautiful too.
Do I . . . know you?
(Is my English better?)

Raymond?!? You're still here! How did you—
Come here,
follow me.
(Ah Duo told me things are better now at NYCI.
After I was let go I met a guy at an Internet cafe back home who recommended me for a gold farming job.)

(These guys were looking for someone with English experience, and I told them I had a degree.)
But you don't!

(It's okay, I was convincing! Nobody else is any better. I picked up a lot from you.)

Oh my god, Raymond!

I was so worried about you. I didn't know if you were okay, if you moved home, or if you're hurt.
It's weird. You're just a collection of pixels, but I worried.

(This life is real too. We're communicating aren't we?)

(Check it out though, at this place we get to build up avatars so we can farm in the upper levels. We actually go on raids together!)
Wow.
(I'm planning again. Now that I'm spending more work time at play I'm thinking I can spend more of my own time studying. Learn more English. Keep moving up in the world.)
So I'm not gonna see you around much then.
(Not as much, yeah.)
I'm going to miss you. But good luck.
Thanks.
(You know, I'm actually not working right now? It's Chinese New Year, which means everyone is on vacation for two weeks.)
Yeah?

Hey, Andaaaaa! Let's blow this thing!

Quit flirting and come raid with us!

Let me introduce you to my friends.

SLEEP

EXIT

SQUARE FISH
An imprint of Macmillan Publishing Group, LLC
175 Fifth Avenue, New York, NY 10010
fiercereads.com

In Real Life was adapted from a story by Cory Doctorow called "Anda's Game" first published on Salon.com in 2004. "Con/Game" was first published on Tor.com.
 Printed in China by 1010 Printing International Limited, North Point, Hong Kong.

ISBN 978-1-250-14428-7 (paperback)

Originally published in the United States by First Second
First Square Fish edition, 2018
Book designed by Colleen AF Venable
Square Fish logo designed by Filomena Tuosto

10 9 8 7 6 5

AR: 3.3 / LEXILE: GN390L

Keep reading for an original comic set in the world of

by author Cory Doctorow and cartoonist Jen Wang.

ORIGINALLY PUBLISHED ON TOR.COM

YOUR ACCOUNT HAS BEEN TERMINATED

Your account in Coarsegold has been terminated for terms of service violations.

"Gold farming" and all related practices are prohibited. These include:

* Using bots for grinding

* Offering or selling in-game gold or items for money ("real-money trading")

* Obfuscating your identity by use of proxies or other

YOUR ACCOUNT HAS

Your account in Co
been terminated f
service violations.

"Gold farming" and
practices are prohi
include:

* Using bots for grin

* Offering or selling in
gold or items for money
trading")

I can't BELIEVE I've got to start over again. What the hell? Terms of service my butt. All they care about is making sure any money spent on Coarsegold goes to THEM.

Bjorn BADARSE? You gotta be kidding me! He's a psycho. AND a racist! You should hear the things he shouts when he's killing gold farmers. He STARTS at "Gook" and it goes downhill from there.

I heard that Coarsegold hired a guy away from the Thundermuggers to run security now. Bjorn Badarse.

You're doomed, dude. What are you going to do about it?

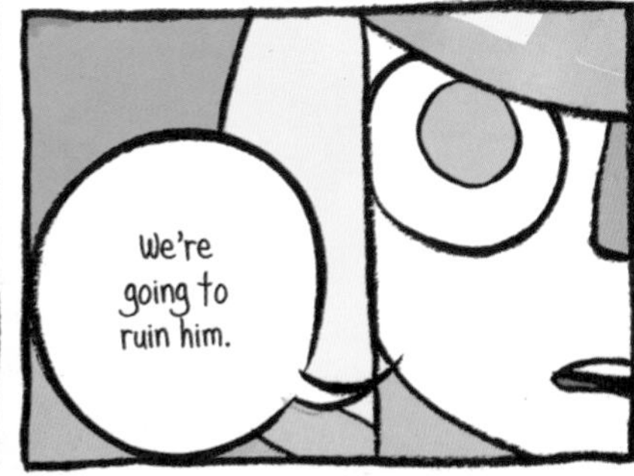

We're going to ruin him.

CON/GAME:

YOU CAN'T CHEAT AN HONEST MAN

WRITTEN BY
CORY DOCTOROW

ILLUSTRATED BY
JEN WANG

THE BUILD-UP

I could get into a lot of trouble for telling you about this. The Fahrenheits would turf my butt.
Yeah, yeah. Come on, what's the deal?

We were running Blonger's Burrow, ten of us. The megaboss was brutal. We tried everything.
Until this noob tried a recurved bow-shot, like level minus bazillion stuff, and croaked it.
So? It's a bug. Report it. Collect a bounty.
You don't understand. AFTER it died, it dropped a Lustigian Broadsword.
And it drops a new one EVERY TIME a noob hits it with a simple arrow. Every. Time.
Only eight of my guildies know about it, including me. We've talked it over. You're the only one who could really exploit this situation properly.
If anyone else tried, Coarsegold management would just shut us down. But you could mine it for swords all day long. They go for over fifty bucks on the darknet auctions!

You're joking. My job is to enforce the rules, not to break 'em.

Come on. No one'll get hurt.

Get out of here. Go on, get lost.

THE CONVINCER

Everyone back; let the noob in!
SHOVE
Go ahead, check it out.

ITEMS FOR

ITEM	PRICE
Bluto's Dagger	$25.00
Lobok	$10.00
Soy Sauce	$5.00
100 Year Egg	$60.00
Lustigian Broadsword	$115.00
Sky Elixir	$3.00
Holdings Axe	$64.00
Shell Rapier	$43.00
Longpo Tusk	$29.00

Half of it is yours by right. Give me your Paypal and I'll transfer it in.
Are you sure?
Course I'm sure. Look, this is the start of a long, fruitful business partnership between Fahrenheits and the Director of Security for Coarsegold.
There're bound to be more sploits like this all over the place. With us scouting them and you running interference for us, we're all in for a very fruitful future.

LUCY
Me too. That was everything I'd ever made in-game. My whole college fund. If this doesn't work, I'm gonna be eating ramen for the rest of my life.

ANDA
My mom'd kill me if she found out.

LUCY
Make sure she doesn't find out.

Sauce	$5.00
00 Year Egg	$60.00
Lustigian Broadsword	$115.00
Sky Elixir	$3.00
Holdings Axe	$64.00

Bad news.

What?

Clan leadership found out about the sploit. It's gonna take a fortune to buy them off. I think the deal is dead.

THE IN-AND-IN
What do you figure they'll want?
Forget it. More than you or I can afford.
Your clan chiefs know the score, right?
Don't worry about how much I can afford. I have ways and means.
Yeah, they got it. But there's another wrinkle.
What?
There's this girl, Kalidestroyer?
What about her?

YOUR ACCOUNT HAS BEEN TERMINATED
Your account in Coarsegold has been terminated for terms of service violations.
"Gold farming" and all related practices are prohibited. These include:
* Using bots for grinding
* Offering or selling in-game gold or items for money ("real-money trading")
* Obfuscating your identity by use of proxies or other
She's pretty senior in the guild, and once she found out it was you—
What?
Look, there's no nice way to say this. She wants your av. You sign it over to her new account, start playing as a noob, or she'll squawk to Coarsegold Inc., and we're all screwed.
Get lost. No. Way.
Think this through, Bjorn. You need a noob to kill the megaboss and you'll be able to swap your swords for a level 80 no problem.
No way.
Look, I've been over this a million times with the Fahrenheits. Kalidestroyer HATES you. I think she's hoping you'll say no so that she can rat us all out.
Forget it.
Think about it, okay?

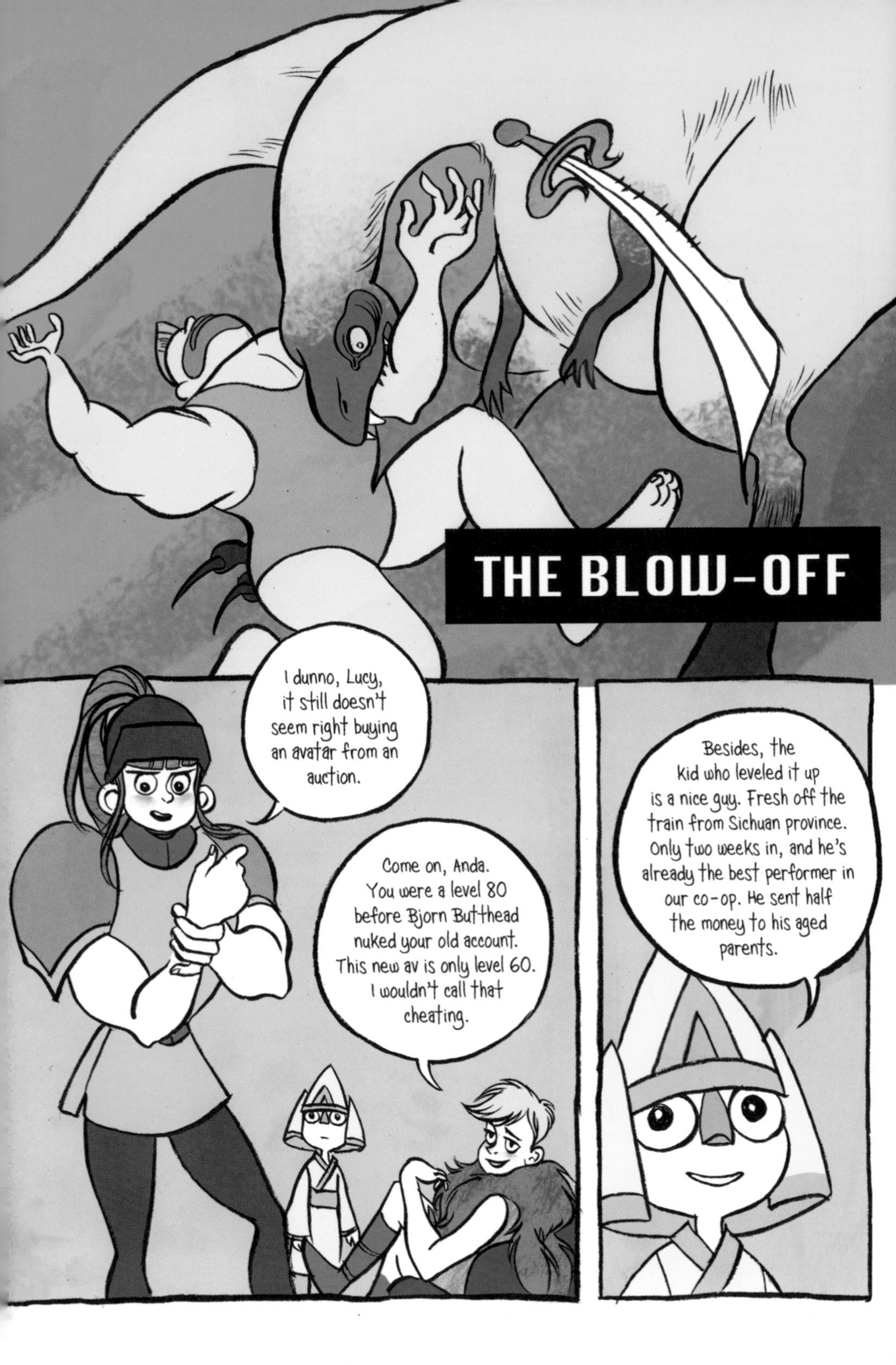
THE BLOW-OFF
I dunno, Lucy, it still doesn't seem right buying an avatar from an auction.
Come on, Anda. You were a level 80 before Bjorn Butthead nuked your old account. This new av is only level 60. I wouldn't call that cheating.
Besides, the Kid who leveled it up is a nice guy. Fresh off the train from Sichuan province. Only two weeks in, and he's already the best performer in our co-op. He sent half the money to his aged parents.

See? Listen to that story and tell me you don't feel all warm inside. TELL ME, you unthinking brute running dog lackey of the oppressors!
Shut up, Sarge.
That's my girl.
I liquidated the gold on one of the internal Chinese-language exchanges. It gets a higher price there. You want your share in your usual Paypals?
I don't want a full share. Just what I had to put in.
Me neither. Raymond, why don't you keep it and buy yourself a replacement av like Anda?
I was already planning to do that before I split the gold! Why don't we give the rest to the co-op?
STORM
NTERTAINMENT
COARSEGOLD ONLINE
NOTICE OF TERMINATION: This is notice of the termination of your employment, effective immediately. You are being terminated with cause, for violating our internal code of conduct regarding the use of unauthorized auction s... ...ade in game...
I want it back, you understand? All of it!
Look, mate, I don't know what to tell you. We're all taking heat for this. Half my clan's been suspended.

The sploit in Blodger's Burrow was working, you saw that. They must have patched it. You know how these things work—
I'm not messing around. You do NOT want to screw with me, you understand?
Have we got a problem, noob?
I don't forget this kind of thing. Watch your back, girl.
Good advice, little boy.
You never know who's behind you.